BY JAMES S. KELLEY

THE SOUTHEAST DIVISION

THE ATLANTA HAWKS

THE CHARLOTTE BOBCATS

THE MIAMI HEAT

THE ORLANDO MAGIC

THE WASHINGTON WIZARDS

The Child's World®

Published in the United States of America by
The Child's World® • 1980 Lookout Drive
Mankato, MN 56003-1705
800-599-READ • www.childsworld.com

ACKNOWLEDGEMENTS

The Child's World®: Mary Berendes,
Publishing Director

The Design Lab: Kathleen Petelinsek,
Design and Page Production

Manuscript consulting and photo research by
Shoreline Publishing Group LLC.

PHOTOS

Cover: Corbis
All interior photos from Reuters except
AP/Wide World: 4, 13, 22, 30

**LIBRARY OF CONGRESS
CATALOGING-IN-PUBLICATION DATA**

Kelley, James S., 1960–

The Southeast division / by James S. Kelley.

    p. cm. — (Above the rim)

Includes index.

ISBN 978-1-59296-985-2
(library bound: alk. paper)

1. National Basketball Association—History—
Juvenile literature. 2. Basketball—Southern
states—History—Juvenile literature. I. Title.
II. Series.

GV885.515.N37K447 2008

796.323'640973—dc22   2007034765

CONTENTS

*On the cover: Dwyane Wade was
a big reason the Miami Heat won
their first NBA title in 2006.*

INTRODUCTION

There hasn't been much suspense to the Southeast Division since it was created during the NBA's major **realignment** in 2004. In each of the division's first three seasons, Miami has won the crown.

The Heat had better watch their rearview mirror, though. That's because division rivals such as the Washington Wizards and the Orlando Magic closed the gap in 2006–07. The Wizards finished just three games back and made the playoffs for the third year in a row; the Magic were four games back and in the postseason again after a three-year absence. Then there are the Charlotte Bobcats and the Atlanta Hawks. Each of those clubs has made big strides recently and feels that it can challenge Miami's supremacy, too.

Maybe the Heat's rearview mirror should come with the standard warning: Objects are closer than they appear!

CHAPTER ONE

THE ATLANTA HAWKS

Hall-of-Famer Bob Pettit led the Hawks to the NBA championship in 1958.

Young fans of the Atlanta Hawks have only seen their team struggle through some difficult seasons. In fact, Atlanta has not had a winning season or reached

They used to call Atlanta's high-flying Dominique Wilkins "the Human Highlight Film." Wilkins was inducted into basketball's Hall of Fame in 2006.

the playoffs since 1999. But what those youngsters may not realize is that the Hawks are one of the NBA's oldest and most historic **franchises**. Their proud tradition even includes an NBA championship in 1958. And with a **core** group of emerging stars leading the way, it won't be a surprise to see the Hawks soon flying high once again.

The Hawks' pro basketball history began in another league and another part of the country in 1946. The team was known as the Tri-City Blackhawks because it represented three neighboring cities on the Mississippi River: Moline and Rock Island, Illinois, and Davenport, Iowa. The Blackhawks originally played in the National Basketball League (NBL), which combined with the Basketball Association of America (BAA) to form the NBA in 1949.

The Blackhawks became the Hawks when they moved to Milwaukee in 1951. In 1955, they packed their bags again and moved to St. Louis. In 13 seasons in St. Louis, the Hawks made the playoffs 12 times. The St. Louis Hawks made the **NBA Finals** in 1957, 1958, 1960, and 1961. In 1958, they won it all, beating the Boston Celtics in six games in the Finals. Bob Pettit was the star of that championship team. He ranked third in the league in both scoring (24.6 points per game) and rebounds (17.4 rebounds per game). Pettit made the All-Star team in each of the 11 seasons that he played in the NBA—all coming with the Hawks—and eventually was inducted into basketball's Hall of Fame.

Pettit retired following the 1964–65 season, and the Hawks moved to Atlanta in 1968. Since then, the Hawks' fortunes have been up and down. In the 1970s, for instance, highly successful seasons were often followed by disastrous ones. In 1977, millionaire broadcaster Ted Turner bought the team. He helped bring consistency back to the Hawks, laying the groundwork for Central Division titles in 1980 and 1987.

Turner's biggest move came in 1982, when he acquired the rights to star forward-guard Dominique Wilkins. A former All-American player at the University of Georgia, Wilkins led the Hawks through the 1980s. He became the team's all-time leader in both scoring and steals. While the Hawks never won an NBA title during this period, they were one of the league's most entertaining teams.

That trend continued in the 1990s. The Hawks made the playoffs seven straight seasons beginning in 1992–93, and they captured the Central Division crown in 1993–94. They equaled a franchise record that year by winning

Red Auerbach coached the Blackhawks to the playoffs in their first season in the NBA in 1949–50. Auerbach later went on to become a Hall-of-Fame legend with the Boston Celtics.

The Hawks unveiled a new logo and color scheme for the 2007–08 season. Their red, white, navy blue, and silver colors are more in line with the original St. Louis Hawks' red, white, and blue. A new Hawks' head logo is more sleek and aggressive.

57 games during the regular season. Key players during this run included Wilkins (who was traded in 1994), center Dikembe Mutombo, and backcourt man Steve Smith.

As good as the franchise was in the 1990s, however, it has been not-so-good in the 2000s. The decade started with a 28-win season in 1999–2000, followed by just a 25-win season in 2000–01. The Hawks finished in last place in their division both of those years.

They bottomed out in 2004–05, winning only 13 games (against 69 losses). They had the worst record in the NBA that season, and the worst in their franchise history.

Help soon was on the way, though. With a squad featuring almost all young players, Atlanta improved to 26 victories in 2005–06, then to 30 wins in 2006–07. Joe Johnson is a veteran guard who still was only 25 years old during the 2006–07 season. He ranked among the NBA's top 10 scorers that year, averaging 25.0 points per game.

Johnson and forwards such as 21-year-old Josh Smith and 20-year-old Marvin Williams have sent the expectations of Hawks' fans soaring!

Joe Johnson averaged a career-best 25.0 points per game in 2006–07 and was an All-Star.

CHAPTER TWO

THE CHARLOTTE BOBCATS

Michael Jordan was the ultimate winner during his best days as a player in the 1990s, when he led the Chicago Bulls to a remarkable six NBA championships. Now he is trying to build a championship team in Charlotte in his current role as the Bobcats' front-office executive in charge of basketball operations.

Jordan played college basketball at the University of North Carolina, in nearby Chapel Hill. The area has always been fanatical about college hoops, but it was left without an NBA team after the Charlotte Hornets moved to New Orleans following the 2001–02 season. The league wasn't going to let down the North Carolina fans, though. By December 2002, the Bobcats' expansion franchise was set to begin play in the 2004–05 season. After a couple of seasons in which the Bobcats struggled in typical expansion fashion, winning only 18 and 26 games, Jordan was brought in to lend his basketball expertise.

In Jordan's first season in 2006–07, the Bobcats won 33 games—the most in

When Robert L. Johnson was awarded the Bobcats' franchise in December of 2002, it marked an historic occasion: He became the first African-American with majority ownership in a major pro sports franchise.

Rejected! Forward Emeka Okafor stops Gilbert Arenas of the division-rival Wizards.

their brief history. Then, after the season, he made some bold moves to try to get the team into the playoffs. First, the club hired former NBA player Sam Vincent as head coach. Vincent, who was an assistant coach with the Dallas Mavericks at the time, has lots of experience as a head coach in international basketball.

One of the first things Vincent did was to let the Charlotte fans know that the team was no longer in its building stage. The franchise intends to win—immediately. "I absolutely, positively anticipate this team making the playoffs, and I would be incredibly discouraged and disappointed if we don't," he said shortly after he was hired as coach.

The Bobcats took a major step in that direction by acquiring the first big-name player in club history, trading for former Golden State guard Jason Richardson on Draft Day, 2007. Richardson was one of the emotional leaders of the Warriors' team that made a surprising run to the playoffs in 2006–07. His best season, though, was 2005–06, when he averaged 23.2 points per game. He has also won the NBA's annual slam-dunk contest twice. The Bobcats traded their first-round draft pick in 2007 (forward Brandan Wright) to Golden State for Richardson and the club's second-round pick (forward Jermareo Davidson).

As a youngster, guard Jason Richardson was a Michael Jordan fan. He wears uniform number 23—the same number Jordan wore while playing for the Chicago Bulls.

Gerald Wallace is one of only three NBA players ever to average more than 2.0 steals and 2.0 blocks in the same season. The others are David Robinson and Hakeem Olajuwon. (Wallace did it during the 2005–06 season.)

Then, just as importantly, the Bobcats re-signed one of their own players. Forward Gerald Wallace, the franchise's all-time leading scorer and a cornerstone of the team since the beginning, could have left as a **free agent** after the 2006–07 season. He averaged a career-best 18.1 points per game that year and could have gotten a lot of money almost anywhere he went. But he decided to stay in Charlotte. "Re-signing Gerald was our top priority," former coach Bernie Bickerstaff, who is now in the team's front office, said.

Wallace joins Richardson, forward Emeka Okafor, center Primoz Brezec, and point guard Raymond Felton to give the Bobcats a talented group of players hungry to become a winning team. And why shouldn't they expect to be winners? Jordan has been successful in just about everything he's done, from his playing days to his role as a businessman.

Bobcats' fans are counting on him having success in the front office, too.

Forward Gerald Wallace has been one of the Bobcats' key players since the beginning of the franchise.

CHAPTER THREE

THE MIAMI HEAT

Step by step, the Miami Heat have become one of the NBA's elite franchises. Step One, they joined the league in the late 1980s. Step Two, they built themselves into a consistent playoff contender in the 1990s. And Step Three, they won their first championship in the 2000s.

The architect of much of the Heat's success has been Pat Riley, who agreed to remain the team's head coach for three additional seasons beginning in 2007–08. Riley originally was hired as the club's president and head coach in 1995—a move that coincided with the Heat's surge to the top of their division. But it wasn't until point guard Dwyane Wade was paired with big man Shaquille O'Neal in 2004–05 that Miami transformed from a good team to a great one.

Before Riley's arrival, Miami had traveled a road that was more or less typical for an expansion team. The Heat entered the league in 1988 and won only 15 games in their first season. Unfortunately, they took a first-year team's troubles to new heights—or depths. Miami set an

Head coach Pat Riley and the Heat celebrate their NBA championship in 2006.

Heat centers Shaquille O'Neal and Alonzo Mourning both rank among the NBA's all-time top 10 in career blocked shots. (O'Neal was eighth entering 2006–07, while Mourning was tenth.)

NBA record by losing its first 17 games. The club finally ended the drought with an 89–88 victory over the Los Angeles Clippers for its first win.

By 1991–92, guard Glen Rice, center Rony Seikaly, and forward Grant Long had put the Heat in the playoffs, albeit with a losing record (38–44). Miami was beaten in the first round by the Chicago Bulls. Two years later, the Heat posted

their first winning season (42–40) but fell to the Hawks in the first round of the playoffs.

It was time to take the next step. So in 1995, Riley came along. He had

It didn't take long for point guard Dwyane Wade to emerge as one of the league's superstars.

As a head coach, Pat Riley has taken his teams to the playoffs 21 times. That's the most in NBA history.

built his coaching reputation by winning four NBA titles with the Los Angeles Lakers. Riley had never missed the playoffs in 13 seasons with the Lakers and the New York Knicks. The streak continued in Miami. A series of off-season moves brought in center Alonzo Mourning and guard Tim Hardaway and shipped out Rice. Mourning led the team in scoring and rebounding while playing a **tenacious** defense. Tough defense was a big part of Riley's teams.

Miami reached the playoffs in each of Riley's first six seasons. The highlight came in 1996–97, when the Heat posted a franchise-record 61 victories, won the first of four consecutive Atlantic Division titles, and advanced to the Eastern Conference Finals before losing to Chicago.

Unfortunately for Miami fans, the Heat could not build on that success in the ensuing seasons, and in 2001–02, the club missed the playoffs for the first time under Riley. Miami's 25–57 record in 2002–03 was its worst since the early days of the franchise, and Riley stepped down as coach (he stayed on as club president) shortly before the 2003–04 season started.

Still, Dwyane Wade was one of the best rookies in the league that year, and the Heat finished 42–40 and made the playoffs. Then, after the season, Miami made huge news. The Heat acquired superstar center Shaquille O'Neal in a trade with the Los Angeles Lakers. O'Neal and Wade gave the Heat a powerful inside-outside combination that led to 59 victories during the 2004–05 regular season. Only a dramatic, seven-game loss to the Pistons in the Eastern Conference Finals kept Miami from advancing to the NBA Finals.

The next season, 2005–06, the team got off to a so-so start, winning a disappointing 11 of its first 21 games. That brought Riley back out of the front office and onto the bench again as coach. Miami went 41–20 the rest of the way and cruised through the playoffs. In the Eastern Conference Finals, the Heat exacted revenge on the Pistons, downing their rivals in six games. Then, in the NBA Finals, Miami dropped the first two games to Dallas and was in danger of losing the third game. But Wade led a fourth-quarter comeback and the Heat went on to win that game and the next three to win their first NBA championship.

With Wade injured and Riley ailing much of the 2006–07 season, the Heat failed to repeat as league champions, but they did win their third consecutive Southeast Division title.

Dwyane Wade was named for his father, Dwayne. But the younger Wade's name was misspelled on his birth certificate!

When center Shaquille O'Neal arrived in Miami, the Heat became instant title contenders.

CHAPTER FOUR

THE ORLANDO MAGIC

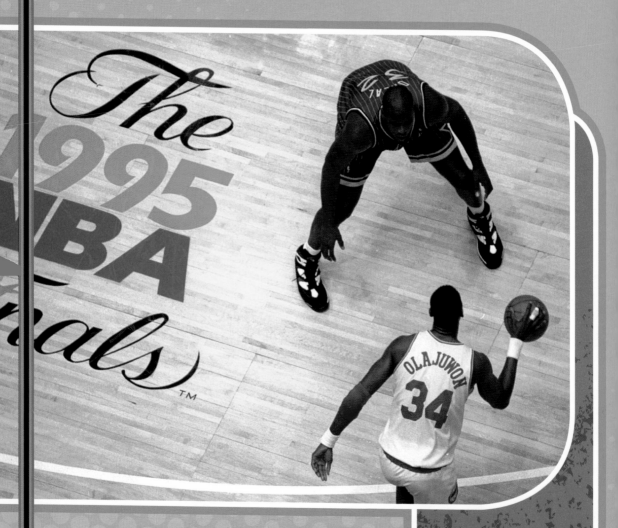

The 1995 NBA Finals™

In just their sixth season (top), the Magic found themselves playing the Rockets in the NBA Finals.

If you charted the history of the Magic, it might look kind of like one of those roller coasters you find at a theme park in Orlando. There was a bit of a lull at first, then a climb that seemed to go straight up followed by a terrifying drop, then a little

Tracy McGrady set a franchise record when he scored 62 points during a 108–99 victory over Washington in March of 2004.

lull again, with a few twists and turns along the way. Now, the Magic's ride seems to be heading upwards again.

Orlando is one of the younger NBA franchises, having entered the league as an expansion team in the 1989–1990 season. The Magic went through an expansion team's typical growing pains, winning just 18 games their first season. That squad had some talent in veterans Reggie Theus and Terry Catledge and rookie Nick Anderson.

After a couple seasons produced 31 wins and 21 wins, the Magic transformed into a playoff contender almost overnight. That's because Orlando drew the first pick in the lottery for the 1992 draft and used the choice to select imposing center Shaquille O'Neal from Louisiana State University.

With O'Neal proving to be a powerful presence on both the offensive and defensive ends of the floor, the Magic improved their victory total by 20 games and finished 41–41 in 1992–93, missing the postseason only by a tiebreaker. O'Neal averaged 23.4 points and 13.9 rebounds and became the first rookie to start in the All-Star Game since Michael Jordan in the mid-1980s.

Because Orlando was the best team in the league that didn't make the playoffs in 1992–93, the club had the worst chance of drawing the number-one slot in the 1993 draft lottery. But the club won the drawing. This time, the Magic selected Michigan forward Chris Webber and then promptly shipped him to the Warriors for guard Anfernee Hardaway. "Penny" was the perfect **complement** to O'Neal. When Orlando added former Bulls forward Horace Grant to the mix the following year, the team was ready to make a run at the NBA championship.

Orlando's 1994–95 team won 57 games on its way to the Atlantic Division title. The Magic then beat Boston, Chicago, and Indiana in the playoffs to reach the NBA Finals in only the franchise's sixth season of play.

Though the Houston Rockets spoiled Orlando's title hopes, the Magic had made a dizzying climb from the bottom of the standings. But O'Neal soon departed to the Los Angeles Lakers as a free agent, and Orlando's fortunes tumbled as quickly as they rose. Not even another superstar in forward Tracy McGrady, who signed with the club in 2000, could stop the Magic's slide. By 2003–04, despite McGrady's second consecutive league scoring title, Orlando won only 21 games and finished in last place in the Atlantic Division.

That convinced the Magic to rebuild. McGrady was traded to Houston before

Orlando had just 1 of the 66 chances in the lottery drawing for the 2003 draft. Like magic, though, its 1-in-66 chance came up!

the season, and the club selected forward Dwight Howard with the top overall pick of the 2004 draft. That same year, guard Jameer Nelson, another first-round choice, was acquired from Denver.

Orlando improved from 21 victories the previous season to 36 victories in 2004–05, then went back to the future for 2005–06 by hiring Brian Hill to coach

Forward Tracy McGrady was a great scorer on some not-so-good Magic teams.

Forward Dwight Howard was the 2004 national high school player of the year. Teammate Jameer Nelson, a guard, was the national college player of the year that same season.

the team for the second time. Hill was at the helm when the club had its best seasons in the mid-1990s. By 2006–07, the Magic were back in the playoffs again under Hill.

Orlando exited quickly in the first round, as there clearly was still a missing piece. The Magic feel like they might have found that piece when they traded for Seattle forward Rashard Lewis before the 2007–08 season. Lewis, a former All-Star, averaged a career-best 22.4 points along with 6.6 rebounds and 2.4 assists for the SuperSonics in 2006–07.

Along with Howard and Nelson, Lewis gives Orlando a talented threesome around whom to build. Magic fans hope that means the roller-coaster ride is taking them back to the top again—although no one knows for sure what's around the next corner!

Forward Dwight Howard is one of the players that the Magic hope will carry them to new heights.

CHAPTER FIVE

THE WASHINGTON WIZARDS

High-scoring guard Gilbert Arenas earned an All-Star selection for the third year in a row in 2006–07.

The Washington Wizards (then known as the Washington Bullets) won their lone NBA championship in 1977–78. The next season, the club won a division championship and reached the NBA Finals before losing.

In their first 45 years of existence, the Wizards played under six different names in three different cities. They began as the Chicago Packers in 1961–62, then changed their name to the Chicago Zephyrs the next season. In 1964, the team moved to Baltimore and became the Bullets, and a decade later the Bullets moved to Washington, D.C. Since moving to the nation's capital, the team has been known as the Capitol Bullets, the Washington Bullets, and, since 1998, the Washington Wizards.

In nearly 30 seasons since, the franchise has not come close to such success. But there are plenty of reasons for Wizards' fans to believe that the team is a lot closer to those championship days than they have been at any other time since.

Two of those reasons are high-scoring guard Gilbert Arenas and versatile forward Caron Butler. Arenas finished third in the league when he averaged 28.6 points per game in 2006–07. Butler added 19.5 points and 7.6 rebounds per game. Both players made the All-Star team. They help provide the Wizards with a nucleus as talented as any since the club's championship season in 1978.

In that title-winning year, six different players averaged more than 10 points per game, topped by forward Elvin Hayes' 19.7 points per game. Hayes, a first-round draft choice in 1968 who was traded to the Bullets in 1972, added 13.3 rebounds per game. He would go on to become the franchise's all-time leading scorer.

After winning 44 games during the regular season, Washington eliminated Atlanta, San Antonio, and Philadelphia in the Eastern Conference playoffs. Then they won a seven-game series over Seattle in the NBA Finals.

That championship was 16 years in the making. That's because the Wizards' franchise first began in Chicago in the

Superstar Michael Jordan was 38 when he came out of retirement to join the Wizards for the 2001–02 season. Jordan averaged 22.9 and 20.0 points in his two seasons with the club, then retired again—this time for good.

Center Wes Unseld and the Bullets were an NBA force in the 1970s.

1961–62 season. After two uneventful years in Chicago produced only 43 victories, a pair of last-place finishes, and few fans, the franchise moved to Baltimore.

Things soon began looking up. In 1967, the club drafted guard Earl "The Pearl" Monroe from Winston-Salem State. The next year, the Bullets selected center Wes Unseld from the University of Louisville. Along with veterans such as high-flying forward Gus Johnson, the pieces were in place for the most successful period in club history.

The stretch began when the Bullets had their first winning season, going 57–25 in 1968–69. It was the first of 10 winning seasons in 11 years and marked the start of 12 consecutive playoff appearances. Though the 1968–69 team was swept out of the playoffs by New York, the Bullets would reach the NBA Finals four times in the 1970s. The last was in 1978–79, when their bid for a second consecutive title was stopped by the Seattle SuperSonics.

Washington managed a few winning seasons shortly after that, but then tumbled into a long period of decline. From 1987–88 to 1995–96, Washington had nine consecutive losing seasons, including three last-place finishes. In 1998–99, the team won only 18 games. In 2000–01, the Wizards managed only 19 victories.

In a game against the Knicks in 2005–06, guard Gilbert Arenas scored 46 points while playing only 30 of the game's 48 minutes. That was the most by a player in league history who played 30 or fewer minutes in a game.

Not even the amazing Michael Jordan could take the Wizards back to the playoffs in the early years of the new millennium. Jordan had led the Chicago Bulls to six NBA championships before retiring following the 1997–98 season. He came out of retirement in 2001 to help the Wizards. Jordan averaged more than 20 points per game in two seasons in Washington. The Wizards came close to the playoffs, but couldn't quite make it in. Then Jordan retired again after the 2002–03 season.

Finally, the Wizards broke through in 2004–05 to win 45 games and make their first playoff appearance since 1996–97. In the playoffs, the Wizards beat Chicago for their first win in a postseason series since the early 1980s. Washington's season ended against Miami in the next round, but the Wizards have been back to the playoffs each year since.

With Arenas and Butler injured in the 2007 postseason, Washington had little chance against the eventual conference-champion Cleveland Cavaliers. Forward Antawn Jamison and the rest of the team did their best, but Cleveland won in a sweep.

Caron Butler is a versatile forward who has Wizards' fans excited about the future.

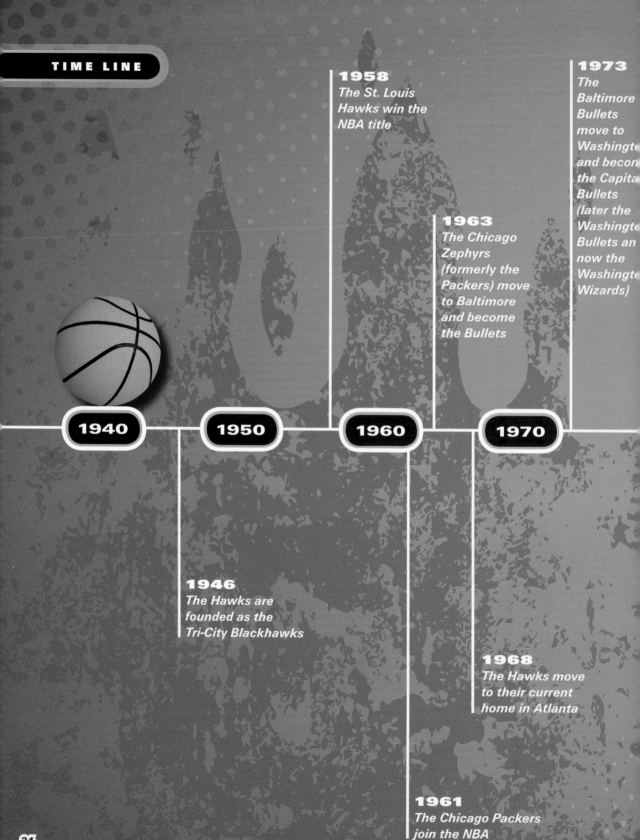

1958
The St. Louis
Hawks win the
NBA title

1963
The Chicago
Zephyrs
(formerly the
Packers) move
to Baltimore
and become
the Bullets

1973
The
Baltimore
Bullets
move to
Washingto
and becon
the Capita
Bullets
(later the
Washingto
Bullets an
now the
Washingto
Wizards)

1940

1950

1960

1970

1946
The Hawks are
founded as the
Tri-City Blackhawks

1968
The Hawks move
to their current
home in Atlanta

1961
The Chicago Packers
join the NBA

1988
Miami begins play as an expansion team

1995
Orlando reaches the NBA Finals in only its sixth season

2005
Miami wins the Southeast in the division's first year of existence

1980   **1990**   **2000**   **2010**

1989
Orlando begins play as an expansion team

2006
The Heat win their first NBA championship

1978
Washington wins its lone NBA title

2004
The Charlotte Bobcats debut as the NBA's 30th team

TEAM RECORDS
(through 2006–07)

TEAM	ALL-TIME RECORD	NBA TITLES (MOST RECENT)	NUMBER OF TIMES IN PLAYOFFS	TOP COACH (WINS)
Atlanta	2,239–2,345	1 (1957–58)	36	Richie Guerin (327)
Charlotte	77–169	0	0	Bernie Bickerstaff (77)
Miami	756–770	1 (2005–06)	12	Pat Riley (426)
Orlando	700–744	0	9	Brian Hill (267)
Washington	1,713–2,016	1 (1977–78)	24	Gene Shue (522)

MEMBERS OF THE NAISMITH MEMORIAL NATIONAL BASKETBALL HALL OF FAME

ATLANTA

PLAYER	POSITION	DATE INDUCTED
Red Auerbach	Coach	1969
Walt Bellamy	Center	1993
Hubie Brown	Contributor	2005
Walter Brown	Contributor	2005
Clifford Hagan	Guard/Forward	1978
Alex Hannum	Coach	1998
Connie Hawkins	Forward	1992
Red Holzman	Coach	1986
Bob Houbregs	Forward/Center	1987
Clyde Lovellette	Center	1988
Bobby McDermott	Guard	1988
Ed Macauley	Forward/Center	1960
Moses Malone	Center	2001
Pete Maravich	Guard	1987
Slater "Dugie" Martin	Guard	1982
Bob Pettit	Forward/Center	1971
Andy Phillip	Coach	1961
Lenny Wilkens	Guard/Coach	1989
Dominique Wilkins	Forward/Center	2006

ORLANDO

PLAYER	POSITION	DATE INDUCTED
Dominique Wilkins	Forward/Guard	2006

SOUTHEAST DIVISION CAREER LEADERS
(through 2006–07)

TEAM	CATEGORY	NAME (YEARS WITH TEAM)	TOTAL
Atlanta	Points	Dominique Wilkins (1982–1994)	23,292
	Rebounds	Kevin Willis (1984–1994)	7,256
Charlotte	Points	Gerald Wallace (2004–07)	2,920
	Rebounds	Emeka Okafor (2004–07)	1,813
Miami	Points	Glen Rice (1989–1995)	9,248
	Rebounds	Rony Seikaly (1988–1994)	4,544
Orlando	Points	Nick Anderson (1989–1999)	10,650
	Rebounds	Shaquille O'Neal (1992–96)	3,691
Washington	Points	Elvin Hayes (1972–1981)	15,551
	Rebounds	Wes Unseld (1968–1981)	13,769

WASHINGTON

PLAYER	POSITION	DATE INDUCTED
Walt Bellamy	Center	1993
Dave Bing	Guard	1990
Elvin Hayes	Forward	1990
Bailey Howell	Forward	1997
Moses Malone	Center	2001
Earl Monroe	Guard	1990
Wes Unseld	Center	1988

CHARLOTTE AND MIAMI

Note: Charlotte and Miami do not have any members of the Hall of Fame (yet!).

ABOUT THE AUTHORS

James S. Kelley is the pseudonym for a group of veteran sportswriters who collaborated on this series. Among them, they have worked for *Sports Illustrated*, the National Football League, and NBC Sports. They have written more than a dozen other books for young readers on a wide variety of sports.